CULT

HARD TIME, BOOK 3

EREC STEBBINS

TWICE PI PRESS

Only one thing is impossible for God: to find any sense in any copyright law on the planet.—Mark Twain

This book is a work of fiction. Any references to historical events, real people, or real locales are used fictitiously. Other names, characters, places, and incidents are the product of the author's imagination, and any resemblance to actual events or locales or persons, living or dead, is entirely coincidental.

Content Guide

This novel contains depictions and references to events and ideas that some will find disturbing, possibly including, but not limited to, monsters, gore, death, torture, captivity, severe illness, pain, fear, medical procedures, and violence. There is also profanity and strong language, the challenging of some accepted norms, and the questioning of different kinds of authority, religious and secular. The book may also contain religion, Oxford commas, and an unnecessary number of tpyos and, grammer misteaks. Readers are asked to prepare accordingly.

1

ANGEL

Electricity cracked. Red sands exploded. A wide and deep depression erupted without visible cause. Individual craters within filled with massive, metallic spheres.

Superheated air drove a wave of punishing thunder across the burning surface of the desert. An undulating dance of grains tapered off hundreds of feet outside the blast radius. Sand rained with the sound of fish frying.

Above, a tumid sun hung heavy and hot over the blistered land. Its malignant sadism baked the tortured wasteland in a crimson glare. Around the new depression, lodged in the goo of liquified sand, a sea of pink bones glinted. Tendrils of fog climbed over the broad anomaly.

Minutes passed. A hatch opened on one of the

mirrored spheres. The smooth, glassy surface fissured as a panel rose toward the looming red eye. Scorched air rushed inside greedily, seeking out raw and uncooked meat. It was met with metal and plastic. Suited bipeds exited the alien structure, reflective faceplates obscuring what lay within the helmets. Rotating their bodies to angle the mirrored visors, three shapes surveyed the landscape.

"This can't be right."

Voices crackled from speakers on the suits.

"Coordinates, temporal and spatial, match, Acolyte Omar Khan."

There was a pause.

"Yes, Elder Saraki, but...what is this? This endless sand?" The visor tipped downward and pitched around them. "Sand and...and bones! Beg the Maker! A lake of bones." The helmet tracked the stream of skeletal remains toward the horizon. His voice trailed in static. "A river of bones."

Saraki recited. "*The hand of the Lord came upon me and brought me out in the Spirit of the Lord, and set me down in the midst of the valley; and it was full of bones. And He said to me, 'Son of man, can these bones live?'*"

"Ezekiel 37," answered Khan.

"So it would seem," said Saraki.

Khan spun toward him. "But, Elder. Where is the Kingdom?"

A higher pitched voice spoke. "It is as was foretold it would pass at Har-Magedon. *'My decision is to gather nations, to assemble kingdoms, to pour out on them My indignation, all My burning anger; For all the Earth will be devoured by the fire of My zeal.'*"

Elder Saraki nodded with his helmeted suit. "The Kingdom awaits, no doubt, or have we lost our faith? But Acolyte Kayla Pier is correct. Remember the Scriptures, The Book of Transformation, *'And lo! Like lava from the depths of Earth, a great fire purged the lands and rid the world of man's evil, preparing the way for the New Creation.'*"

Muffled howls escaped from the distal sphere. The three pivoted toward it, shivering despite the furnace around them. The sounds were unearthly.

"And we bring the New Creation," said Saraki, turning to the other spheres. "Enough. We have a quest. Check pods two and three. What keeps the others?"

Acolytes Pier and Khan shuffled in the heavy gear, one to each silvered sphere. Tapping on control strips running along their arms, they opened the doors and entered.

Saraki surveyed the barren desert.

"Great Master," he whispered, "remember we are only dust. Shine your mercy on our sinful weakness."

Pier exited the far sphere and stumbled across the sand toward Saraki.

"Elder, the Angel of pod three is safe." She hesitated. "It demands food."

Saraki stared forward into the emptiness. "Your Kingdom come. *Soon*." He turned to the middle sphere. "Where is Khan?"

Moments later, Khan emerged. He stood a moment in the doorway, frozen in place, head tilted down. He pushed forward, white boots tacky from the congealing sand. He did not speak as he approached.

"Status?" barked Saraki.

Khan cleared his throat. "There has been a neutrino field failure of the pod, Elder." His voice was flat through the speakers. The mirrored visor pointed blankly at the other two.

Saraki straightened. "How bad?"

"Entropy beyond fifty percent nominal."

"The Maker help us. What's left of them?"

"Some are vegetables. Brain monitors in alarm. A few are cogent. But they appear to retain no useful memories. Only Acolytes Maryam Ford and Aruna Sodhi appear relatively intact."

"Bring them here, both of you."

It took thirty minutes. The acolytes vanished within the middle pod. After the delay, they led two shaky figures toward Saraki. The Elder had busied himself erecting a monitoring station, complete with sensors, antenna, and a reflective tent. He grumbled as the wobbly new pair approached.

"Inside, all of you."

Within the tent, Elder Saraki removed his helmet. The others followed his lead. His gray braids were disheveled. Purple irises lurked in a deep squint from the heat and sandy air. His black skin began to sweat.

"Breaking protocol for a moment. This environment is hostile beyond expectations. Suits stay on as much as possible." He glanced between them. "But we need to talk. Eye to eye. Window to the soul." They stared at him. "We have suffered a great loss."

Acolyte Pier lowered her head, beaded dreadlocks concealing her face, the flash of purple extinguished. As all the Believers, Acolyte Khan also sported the unusual eyes. He stared at Saraki with raised brows, his dark hair matted and brown skin flushed. They each propped the other two travelers.

Khan held the bald, olive-skinned Maryam Ford. Pier draped the arm of Aruna Sodhi over his shoulders, her waist-length hair tangled in his suit.

"Initial scans report dangerous radiation levels," began Saraki. "Even with the suits, it is hazardous to remain outside for long. We must find shelter."

"But where?" asked Khan.

"Scans also report electromagnetic frequencies consistent with human transmissions. They are oddly coded, and the AI has been unable to decrypt them as yet."

Pier raised her head, lines creasing her dark forehead. "Why would the Kingdom not use protocol?"

Saraki grimaced. "Because the transmissions are likely not from the Kingdom." He held his hands up as they murmured. "Humans have been sent here for tens of thousands of years. Most we know little about. Fear not—we will find the Kingdom." He held their gaze. "Now, Acolyte Sodhi. Why are you here?"

Sodhi's mouth hung open, her copper skin slick with perspiration. Her eyes struggled to focus on Saraki. "Engineer. Yes. I'm an engineer. Life support. Grade Six. For the Kingdom. For the Angels." Her face hardened. "We are Mission 4003. Perhaps the last."

"Why the last?"

"Negotiations have failed." Her voice grew in confidence. "War seemed inevitable."

Saraki nodded. "You are fortunate to have your mind, Acolyte Sodhi." He turned to the other woman. "And you? What do you remember?"

Ford vomited. A spray of pink splashed on the sands inside the tent, splattering their suit legs. They stepped backward, the radius of their circle increasing.

"Apologies, Elder Saraki," Ford managed, spitting into the sand. "I'm Corps Engineer Fourth Grade Maryam Ford, Acolyte of the Kingdom and servant of the One True Maker. Our mission is to find the End Times Kingdom. We are to deliver our most advanced Angel and aid in the Final Quest." Her lavender gaze held firm as her body swayed. Sweat beaded on her scalp.

Saraki nodded. "We have lost all our Soldier class but you, Acolyte Ford. The rest of us will have to call upon our Knights' training for any defense required."

Khan frowned. "Defense?"

"Signals show sinners abound. We must be careful until we find the Faithful." His eyes darted toward the tent exit. "And we do not know what else may lie in wait in this terrible place."

Pier nodded. "And the others, Elder Saraki? Most cannot walk. All have significant brain damage, far beyond memory loss."

A sigh escaped the Elder's lips. "They will only burden us and imperil the mission."

Saraki glanced outside at the third sphere. The howls radiating from it were more pronounced, carrying eerily over the sands.

"And the Angel must feed."

He lifted his helmet over his head and locked it in place.

"Master accept our prayers."

Five bulky suits knelt around a thick obelisk. The square base was broad, the height twice their own. A pyramid with blinking lights perched atop the squat object. A rectangular fissure along one face disappeared as the door sealed. The mirrored surface reflected the sands and survival suits like the spheres beside it.

Elder Saraki prayed.

"Lead us to your Kingdom and the Coming Transformation."

Their mirrored images in the structure were stained by a languid stream of blood. Thick and clotting, it dripped down the sides and pooled in the sands. The red fluid flowed from the vanished doorway. It crept across the desert floor to the open hatch of the third sphere. Tattered flesh haphazardly decorated the darkened sands.

"So be it."

The five rose. The tent and sensors were packed and stowed on a levitating craft. Compact, designed to fit within the house-sized spheres, the vehicle held ten people. Supplies filled an expansive storage bed in the back.

Saraki motioned to the obelisk.

"Load the sarcophagus on the glider. We will navigate toward the signals ahead, straight along this road of bones. The carnal mazes of Sodom and Gomorrah await, my children. But doubt not, we will make our way to the Kingdom."

Four moved toward the obelisk, but one halted, staring off into the desert behind them.

"Elder Saraki," called Ford, "something approaches."

The five stared out into the sands. In the distance, several hundred yards away, the sands undulated. A bulge rose within the desert floor, larger than their glider, and sped up the trail of bones. Three other moving mounds joined it, the four packets beneath the grains racing toward them.

Saraki shouted. "Weapons out. Acolyte Ford, do not engage."

"Elder!" Ford spun to face him.

"Do *not* engage. You're still too weak. Acolytes Khan and Pier, intercept and sterilize. Now!"

The pair touched the control strips on their suits. Slots opened in the back to reveal broad cylinders. There was a rush of wind, and the sand beneath them burst into a cloud.

Jets hurled them skyward. They grasped heavy rifles in their arms, bright balls of plasma exploding from the barrels. The blue spheres smashed around the rushing sand mounds, the desert surface rupturing, molten silicon and smoke rising. None found a direct hit. The pair landed a hundred yards beyond their launch point, crouching and aiming at the approaching sand hills. They fired again.

Plasma spheres struck two mounds, sand detonating with flesh. Black limbs flew through the air, severed from something monstrous. The sand mounds fissured, exposing an octopus of arms flailing, their length covered by spikes and razored edges. The bodies were round and obsidian. Their bulks leapt above the Acolytes, who fired vainly at the descending horrors.

Saraki grabbed his rifle. "Dear Maker."

The forms of Pier and Khan scattered like fragments in a blender. A cloud of red misted in the distance around them. A high-pitched shriek from Pier died over the sands.

The monsters dove back beneath the desert. The mounds rushed forward.

"What are they?" cried Sodhi, the rifle trembling in her arms.

"Demons," whispered Ford, down on one knee, her rifle pointed toward the rushing things.

"Demons we lesser creatures cannot defeat," said Saraki.

He turned toward the obelisk. Howls escaped as the broad structure shook. He glanced back at the incoming mounds, now fifty yards away.

"The Angel is roused. It senses these abominations."

Ford fired. Blue plasma balls flashed away like maniacal will-o'-the-wisps. One set hit and the black nightmare ruptured in the distance. Its limbs twitched while the remaining three creatures rocketed forward.

Saraki lurched toward the obelisk and placed his hand against a glowing panel on the side. He screamed, his eyes wide.

"Arise and vanquish your enemies!"

Light flashed from the structure. Saraki crouched and shielded his eyes. A thunderous impact rattled the landscape as a white blur hurtled into the cresting black waves.

Sand pelleted their suits, the sky itself darkening from a cloud of granular precipitate thrown to the heavens. Slaps of compressed air struck them, one knocking Sodhi on her side. Ford shouted through the speakers, the amplifiers powerless over the turbulence.

"I can't see! What's happening!"

No one answered. Inhuman cries tore through the turmoil. The ground shook.

Silence fell.

The brown cloud showered the sweltering desert in rough curtains. The mayhem had scratched even the synthetic materials of their suits, the visors etched and their visibility degraded. The red eye reached downward again, the humans feeling its burn once more.

"It's over," gasped Saraki.

Ford aimed toward the shrinking dust cloud. Sodhi limped to a stand, propping herself on a rifle. Saraki stepped beside them, gazing over the sand.

The clearing debris revealed three black heaps. The monstrous forms of razored tentacles were strewn and mangled. One had been ripped in two.

Ford lowered her weapon. Blood lay like a lake around the corpses.

"The Maker have mercy."

White feathers dyed crimson spread over the black shapes, the wingspan a tent obscuring both predator and prey. The feathered thing shook as its concealed front lunged into the black creature.

"It feeds," said Sodhi.

"And thank the Maker for it," said Saraki. "It will eat beyond its fill, and give us more time."

Ford nodded. "Maybe we can get it back inside without the neural safeties."

"Perhaps," said Saraki. He turned to the glider. "But give the Angel its space. Acolyte Ford, you will observe and report. Prepare us when it finishes."

"Yes, Elder," Ford said, her visor unmoving, pointed at the carnage behind them.

"Acolyte Sodhi, you will assist me in locking the navigation to the signal."

Sodhi stood still and silent. A statue.

Saraki turned his survival suit toward her. "I know you both have trauma from the transit. We have suffered devastating losses. Now three must do the work of thirty. We must ferry our charge to the Kingdom. We must call on the Creative Spirit to strengthen us." His voice rose. "Are you with us, Acolyte Sodhi?"

The figure shook. "Yes. Yes, of course, Elder. Forgive me."

"You are forgiven," said Saraki, returning to the glider. "Now come and assist me."

"What of these hell creatures?" Ford asked, the wet pops of chewed flesh reaching their ears. "It can't eat them all."

Saraki didn't turn as he climbed into the glider. "The fire above will purge them. Let God add them to the bones."

3

SINNER

F ord removed the scope adaptor from her visor plate. She pocketed the device and sealed the suit.

"It's a small dome, Elder. The bigger one's a day's ride on the glider. At least."

Saraki crouched beside her and Sodhi. "The people you saw—you're sure they spotted us?"

"Definitely," said Ford. "They're on some kind of caterpillar, treads rolling toward us. One waved."

"Waved?" He scowled. "Master give us strength."

The three sat on the crest of a towering dune, hundreds of feet above the shimmering desert floor. A glint of light flashed from a small structure some distance behind the approaching craft. The shadow of a much larger construction hung on the horizon.

"We could evade," said Sodhi. "Lose them in the desert."

Saraki shook his head. The cruel sun sank toward the surface of the world, its deep red flickering across his mirrored visor.

"It'd be foolish. We don't know if we can outrun them. More importantly, we may need them. They follow this bone road. It seems to run its awful course to the buildings we see. Every cursed thing in this hell follows this path."

Sodhi pressed. "Which is why we should avoid it!"

"And go where, Acolyte Aruna Sodhi? I see nothing in any other direction to the horizon. We're only three. We've lost most of our brothers and sisters, their company, their expertise. We need water. The Angel needs water. Where there are settlements, there is water. The Kingdom must be that way as well."

Ford checked the settings on her weapon. "So, we meet them?"

"It would appear so." Saraki punched the control strip on the glider. The sand sprayed out beneath them. "That devil's eye is setting. Let's get to that small dome before nightfall. Who knows what prowls this wasteland after dark."

The glider tipped and raced down the dune.

"Whoa! Hold up," came the muffled shout from the burlap bag in front of them.

Metal gleamed in the hood, a conical and porous grill at the mouth, glassy ovals embedded in metal rings where eyes might reside. The thick material of the suit stretched as the man held two arms in the air. One ended with a weapon.

A group of armed sacks around him aimed weapons their way, fifteen at least. The troop leapt off their desert roller and approached, fingers on triggers.

"You arrivals?" said the man.

Another suited sack pushed to the front, a tone of command in his voice.

"Yo, rookie, look at that gear. High-end Late Era. See there, Donner? Environ suits, heavy duty. Energy weapons. Definitely arrivals. Gilded mother-fuckers."

Saraki scowled and whispered on their private suit channel.

"Sinners. Be on your guard."

Ford and Sodhi kept their weapons aimed.

"Their weapons are primitive, Elder," said Ford. "Low power metal hurlers. Might not even pierce our suits."

"Patience, Acolyte Maryam Ford. I remind you, we need these people. Until we find word of the Kingdom and the Faithful."

Ford exhaled. Saraki spoke over the speakers.

"We are glad to make your acquaintance. Yes, indeed, we are newly arrived. We seek shelter and offer you our company."

Laughter bubbled from the baggy group.

The commanding voice among them nodded. "Nice to make your acquaintance, too. *Professor.*" More laughter. "I'm Lang Zheng, boss of this pack of walking dead. We're a scouting party. Basically we ride the grains, run from squids, and pick up clueless arrivals like you. Guide them to the Waypoint."

"What's the Waypoint?" asked Saraki.

"Brand new dome. Dome number two in hell." He laughed. "Stock and heal up before hopping a transport to the Great Dome."

"I see. Thank you. We accept your help gladly."

"Mmmm-hmmm," grunted Lang. "But first, we got some protocol to follow. Need to inspect your craft." He glanced at the bed of the glider. "Nice tech there. Interesting stuff."

"Is this necessary?"

The weapons before them twitched.

"'Fraid so." The hood with the glassy eyes tilted to one side. "Before that, I'm gonna have to ask you to raise your visor."

Saraki stiffened. "You can't be serious. It's dangerous!"

"Dangerous? More like deadly. But your suits ain't gonna save your asses. That red light eats into you no matter what. A little direct ain't gonna make a difference. 'Sides, it's sunset." The shape reached burlap arms to his neck and twisted. "Here, I'll start."

A loud click and rush of air accompanied the hood removal. A deeply bronzed man, wrinkled like an octogenarian sporting sun-bleached hair, stared back. He wore special lenses, his cornea milky.

"Unacceptable, Elder!" came a hiss on the private com from Ford.

"Silence," returned Saraki. He stared at the weapons around them. He gazed down the long bone road in the unforgiving desert.

Lang spoke again. "You weren't wrong, professor, it's a punishment on naked skin out here." He nodded to the troop behind him. They took a step closer, weapons high. "Visor up, please. *Now.*"

The visor on Saraki's suit clicked and scrolled upward with a hiss. The old man's smooth dark skin clashed with the cracked leather of Lang's.

Saraki squinted. Even with the star approaching the horizon, its malice burned his face. He spoke through gritted teeth.

"I am Namadi Saraki. We have met with great tragedy on arrival, or our numbers would be much greater."

Lang squinted, adjusting buttons on his heavy lenses. "Ta ma de! It's the fucking cult."

The scout Donner shuffled his feet behind Lang. "Cult? You mean the ones from the war?"

"Before your time, I know. But it's them."

Ford and Sodhi angled their helmets toward Saraki. The old man said nothing.

"How'd you know?" asked Donner.

"Look at those eyes. Ain't no other Norms got purple eyes. The cult went all in on designer genes."

Ford couldn't stop herself. "Cult? Is that how you refer to us, you heathens? We're *Apostles*. You know our rightful name. We've sent many before us. We have important work."

Lang smiled, reattaching his hood. "You're a little behind the times."

The scouts around laughed.

Donner shook his head. "Good one, sir."

"Listen to 'em. Still think they run the place. *Important work.*" Lang's face vanished behind the burlap, his voice muffled again. "Not no more. Civil war ended all that."

Saraki startled, his magenta eyes sparkling in the setting sun. "Civil war?"

"Might want to raise the fancy visor, professor," said Lang.

Saraki frowned. The reflective surface scrolled down and covered his face. His skin stung.

Lang sighed. "Bloods and Cults. War was about the damn end of us." The hood moved back and forth. "Gonna be an adjustment for you folks. But count yourselves lucky. Few years ago, we would've shot you on sight. But we need the hands."

"What are you talking about? Where are the Apostles?"

"Mostly dead, grandpa. You might find a few at the Waypoint, more at the Great Dome. They're a sorry bunch now. But that ain't my concern." He stared at the vehicle bed. "But something else is."

The glass-eyed hood flicked from his scouts to the glider. They fanned out, weapons aimed in a semicircle around the arrivals. Lang shuffled through the sand to the sarcophagus in the back of the truck. The obelisk lay on its side for transport.

"What you got in that box interests the hell out of me."

Saraki's voice crackled from his suit's speakers. "Private matters. Let it be."

"Don't fuck with us, professor. That's a Trune."

The three Apostles said nothing to the men. Their internal coms buzzed.

"They know!" said Sodhi.

"They'll take the Angel!" cried Ford. "Should we engage?"

Saraki felt dizzy. They were on a knife's edge. He couldn't let them harm the Angel. Yet without the dome ahead, he knew they were doomed.

"Hold!" he hissed. "If they touch the sarcophagus, kill them all. Otherwise, follow my lead."

Lang looked between the three. "God damned Apostles. Bloods outnumbered you. All those endless arrivals. But you had your fucking WMDs." Lang slung his weapon to his shoulder. "Well, you'll learn the new order. And you'll see what we do with Trunes here now. But if you want to live, you'd better get to shelter. Waypoint's just ahead. You can get a transport there to the Dome."

Ford broke Saraki's enforced silence. "We don't need your help."

Lang scoffed. "Listen, holy roller, you're new here. My condolences. But let me spell it out for you. There's two places with water in hell, and you won't get gettin' in either one without us. I see your weapons. Nice plasma shit. Probably cook us before we can get through those suits. Probably. But then your asses are fried. Domes'll lock you out. Then the fucking squids will have you for dinner."

"Say nothing, Acolyte Maryam Ford," said Saraki.

She ignored him. "Squids? Those tentacled things? We don't need you. We killed four of them."

Lang chuckled. "Did you now?" He looked at the obelisk. "Those guns are good, but they're not that good. You're not that fast. But I've seen some Trunes take out a squid or two. I bet you had some help."

"Maybe we did," said Ford.

Saraki howled on the internal channel. "Silence!"

Lang didn't move, his weapon resting on his shoulder as he stared into the front of Ford's weapon.

"Isn't that interesting. You might just fetch a real reward for that one."

Blasphemy. Saraki ground his teeth.

Lang continued. "Still doesn't solve your water problem. Believe me, sister, there ain't a drop on the surface. And it don't look like you have the hardware to dig."

Donner leaned in toward Lang, the leader nodding underneath his hood.

"Besides, I think the Waypoint's your place. Someone there you might want to meet."

Saraki shook his head. "What do you mean? Who?"

"A *real* prophet. So they say. Not your cultist bull-shit. Talks to *God*. Predicts the fucking future." He slung his weapon down and motioned to the road of bones. "Come with us and meet her."

"Her?"

"The Woman. Arrived at the Waypoint two days ago from her preaching at the Great Dome. Heard her some time back. She's all on about finding the damned Ark of the Covenant."

Lang turned and his team followed him to their vehicle. A wind stirred, swallowing his words in the rasping sand.

"What are you waiting for? Dome's got God and water."

4

PROPHET

L ang escorted them along the cursed road of bones to the sparkling half-sphere. Figures perched along its surface and construction rang over the desert, the dome still in the final stages of completion.

Corpses of men and monsters littered the final distance from the dunes across this short, flat patch of desert. Some fresh and stinking. Many rotting or desiccated.

More bones. Saraki raised his gaze and tried to ignore the mangled forms.

Rows of machinery, some if it wrecked as if by the onslaught of giants, lined the path. Weapons atop the diverse and haphazard constructions were manned by more brown sacks of burlap.

Lang paraded them between rows of armored

units. "Need the cover. Squids can smell the mass of meat inside."

Saraki scowled. "Meat?"

"*Us*. Getting worse as we fill the dome. Drives 'em nuts. The Great Dome's too big, and we got sentries all around. But out here it's different. Smaller. New. We get three or four quads a day making a run at it. Don't know what these monsters eat when they can't get human."

"What *do* they eat?"

Lang's burlap hood shook back and forth. "Hell if I know. Rumors only. Other shit under the sand, shielded from that ball of death. Small things. Bigger things. Who the fuck knows?"

The guards joined Lang's scouting party. Their growing numbers made escape impossible. Conversation outside was brief. They approached the dome, the doorways opened, and the group was shepherded inside.

Then the helmets came off and the gasps began. Silence fell. A swelling chorus of whispers followed like some angry hornets' nest.

"Ignore these lost souls," muttered Saraki to his Acolytes, averting his eyes from the glaring faces.

"We don't see too many cultists, anymore," chuckled Lang, his leathered face beaming at Saraki.

Ford and Sodhi scowled but kept silent.

Saraki tried to redirect the attention from the gawking onlookers. "What rank are you, Lang? A commander? I can tell you're a soldier."

"Just a Norm scout," said Lang. "Nothin' like no commander."

Saraki's purple eyes squinted. "How old are you?"

"Thirty-two. Got a few more years in me before something breaks for good. Maybe." He laughed at Saraki's expression. "We don't age so well here, professor. Ain't many gray-hairs around 'less they arrived old, like you."

A muscled man slapped Lang on the soldier. "Nice haul, Zheng. You'll get a bonus for this."

Saraki approached the man. "Excuse me, I am—"

"Save it, fanatic," spit the guard. "Keep your mouth shut, do what you're told, and we might not throw you in detention." The crowd murmured around them, hostile expressions plentiful.

"Look," said Saraki, licking his lips. "Once we find the faithful, we can recompense..."

"Or I could let these bastards at you."

Saraki paused, avoiding the hateful eyes. He

closed his mouth. The soldiers pointed guns at the heads of the three arrivals.

"Your weapons, God freaks."

They had no choice. They surrendered their arms. Ford muttered constantly under her breath.

"That's some impressive tech," noted the muscled guard. "It's ours now. R&D's going to have a field day at the Dome."

Saraki shook his head. "But we aren't going to the other dome. Just this one. Please, perhaps we can reach some sort of arrangement—"

"Dome's it, friends," interrupted the guard. Other soldiers untied any remaining items from the bed. "What'd they tell you when they launched your asses out here? Don't matter. There's only two places where things live. The desert's got the monsters. We got the domes. This one's a way station. Unless you're assigned, you move the hell on."

"Where is the Temple?" asked Saraki. "We're going there."

The guard scrunched his face and looked to Lang, who shook his head.

"He means the Apostles' temples. There ain't many left in the Dome. Not after the war."

Ford's eyes widened. "What happened to it?"

Lang rolled his eyes. "It? There weren't no *it*.

Bunch of them. Bunch wrecked in the fighting. Most of the rest the mobs burned down. Ya'll weren't exactly popular."

Saraki felt his throat tighten. Swallowing hurt.

"What's left?" he whispered.

"Here? Waypoint's got a chapel, I think. No priest. Not many of them left, either. A few under the Great Dome."

Saraki straightened. "Thank you. We'll find it ourselves. Let us take our things and be out of your way."

The guard glowered. "Not with that, you won't. Trune's for quarantine."

"Quarantine? Is there a disease?"

"Yeah," said the guard smirking. "It's called Trunes. We keep them under guard. No way you're toting that thing around the dome."

"It's a biosafe container. We control it."

"Yeah, sure," said Lang. "Like during the war. Your little army of those monsters almost ended everything."

The guard signaled to the other soldiers, who aimed weapons at the Apostles. "It goes with us, or we mow it and any of you down that try to stop us."

Ford and Sodhi stared between their Elder and the soldiers. Saraki's shoulders slumped.

"Chapel's at the center," pointed Lang. "This dome was started before the war ended. Right around the time I arrived. Still had some faithful then."

The soldiers loaded the sarcophagus on a giant dolly, along with all the other contents of the glider.

Lang put his hands on his hips.

"Transport's on a schedule, so don't dally. Plenty of arrival stations. Find one or ask." The corner of his mouth twitched. "Good luck."

He turned and left. The three Apostles watched the men cart their goods, glider, and angel away. The obelisk glowed in the dim light inside the Waypoint.

"What now?" huffed Ford.

Saraki sighed. "We find the sanctuary. And pray."

They met the Woman in front of the chapel.

They searched for hours, even in the small enclosure of the Waypoint. Without maps, without a guide, they were lost. Hostility and near violence met most attempts at communication, their purple eyes a mark of shame and guilt.

They wandered around the camps filled with new arrivals, most injured and horribly burned, medical personnel attending the suffering. They shunned the brothels, the filthy markets, the peddlers of poison and transgression. Twice they stumbled upon quarantine stations filled with Trunes in cages.

"We sent so many," said Sodhi, staring open-mouthed.

"Not only us. Do not forget the war. Or the heretics."

Ford sneered. "These are primitive. Slobbering monsters. The Angel could erase them in moments."

"It took many thousands of years to perfect them," said Saraki. "Many of the imperfect forms were sent here. Many by our enemies."

The creatures screamed and whined, yipped and moaned. Many thrashed against the bars of their cages: bloody, bruised, broken. Some sat still, monstrous forms in meditation. One broke through the metal bars to slaughter several men in a bloodied frenzy before it was put down.

Their Trune hibernated unseen, encased in advanced technology, a contingent of armed guards near. Their purple eyes lingered on the distant sarcophagus.

"We will get the Angel back, of course," said

Saraki. "Once we've made contact with the Faithful. Or if these fools accidentally release it."

"If we can contain it," said Sodhi, terror in her eyes. "Without the sarcophagus, the neuronal feedback...."

Saraki patted her shoulder. "Have faith. God will provide."

At last, a merchant pointed them the way to the chapel. They navigated another wall of medical booths and dying arrivals. The trio stumbled toward a darker and undeveloped section of the dome. The walls towered over them.

The chapel was tiny, the size of a shed, a crumbling sandstone structure erected in haste. A golden Spiral of Progression hung askew from above the doorless entrance. The inside was black and filled with sand, torched from a time of war and hate.

Of persecution, thought Saraki.

In front of the doorway stood a woman.

"The Maker have mercy," chanted Sodhi. She placed her hand on Ford's shoulder and gripped.

The leathered face of Lang had been shocking. But the hag before them was the broth of nightmares. Human skin shouldn't have darkened and mottled and bent so monstrously. Yet it held together, tortured and thickened, beyond comprehension. The wrecked remnants of her eyes hid in overlapping hunks of cragged tissue, pressed into the sockets like some fried egg white. Her pocked scalp was bald. Fire had burned the eyebrows away.

Two shrouded forms attended her on either side. They wore robes with hoods that concealed most of their features. But not all. White hair spilled from the edges of the cowls. Pale hands folded at their chests.

"Synths." Saraki caught his breath. "Master save us."

"You will come to the desert with me," the pruned hump before them bellowed, her voice resonant. The three gaped at her. "And we will find the Ark."

"Who *are* you?" said Ford, her brow a furrowed pinch.

The hag cackled. "Names. I have forgotten my own. Most of us have. But I am called the Woman."

A chill flowed through Saraki. "Leave us be. This is our chapel. We want nothing with you."

"Unholy man, *you will*. You misunderstand your fate. You go to the Dome because it houses the remaining shards of your faith. You will search and find those pathetic remains. You will begin to understand. Then you will come to me."

Ford scoffed. "Why would we come to you, unbeliever? For what?"

"*You* will not. But others will. For deliverance and salvation."

Ford rolled her eyes. "This is ridiculous."

The eyeless sockets froze Saraki. The harsh voice terrified him. "God has revealed to me your purpose. You will see the Ark."

She limped down the short steps from the chapel and approached. The hooded Synths kept to her sides. She stopped inches away, her creviced visage a horror to behold.

"When your hope is gone, when you know your prophecy is misread, remember what I now say: I know of the true Ark, what your scriptures call the Cosmic Vessel. That which seeds universal change."

Saraki stammered. "How, how do you know—"

"Come to me then. Fulfill your prophecies."

Her white eyes tracked across their faces. They shuddered, even as the Woman grinned, revealing toothless gums and breath that stank of decay.

She shambled past them toward the center of the dome. Her voice trailed.

"But first, we must survive the Hunter."

5

ERINYS

At the Woman's last words an explosion shook the dome.

Saraki squinted, a bright light flashing near the doorway they had entered. Screams dusted over him like gusts of wind as automatic projectile discharge rang off the curved ceiling. A tide of bodies scattered toward them.

Hunter?

He turned toward the Woman. She'd vanished. The shrouded Synths, gone. Ford's voice pelleted his ears.

"Elder!" shouted Ford.

She grabbed his suit and turned him.

"There's a battle! We need our weapons!"

The shock subsided, and he stammered, "We don't know where anything is!"

Ford scanned the rushing forms, and powered up her suit. A metallic clack signaled the engagement of the hydraulics, and then she was airborne, pouncing, landing on top of a man rushing past them. He wailed and pushed up.

"Quiet!" she screamed, pinning him to the ground. "Answers! You give them or you die, heathen!"

Eyes wide, the dark man nodded.

Her bald scalp glinted. "What's happening?"

"Hunter!"

"What's a hunter?"

Saraki and Sodhi approached, both planting their feet to steady against the dashing flood. More explosions set the earth trembling. More screams of terror.

"No time!" He struggled to escape. Ford squeezed his arms, drawing a scream. "Stop! Please."

"Tell me!"

"I don't know. Nobody knows. They come. They arrive. Sudden. They kill."

Saraki bent toward him. "Kill you? Why?"

The man's eyes darted, drawn to the sprinting shapes flashing past.

"Not us! Trunes! They come, they kill Trunes.

They only kill us if we try to stop them! If we're in the way. Please! We have to get away from the Trunes!"

Saraki nodded to Ford. "Let him go. We move!"

"The Angel," whispered Sodhi.

Ford yelled at the man, her teeth bared. "Where are our weapons?"

"Your weapons?" The man's face was tight with terror and confusion.

"Let him go!" said Saraki. "He's not a soldier. He won't know. We must get to the Angel."

"And fight this *hunter* with what?" said Ford.

"Suit lasers," said Saraki. "It's all we have."

"We need our rifles!"

"No time!" He set his jaw. "We may need to open the sarcophagus. If we can't defend it, it must defend itself."

Ford nodded and released the man. He stumbled to his feet rushing away, never turning back.

Saraki pointed to the focal point of the noise and fleeing people.

"Whatever it is, it's there. If it is hunting Trunes, the Angel must be close." He powered up his suit and engaged the jets, raising his helmet. "Controlled bursts! Careful of the wall curvature. Eliminate anyone who tries to stop you. Their lives do not matter."

They fitted their helmets. The thrusters screeched on their backs. The three white forms shot into the air.

From above, the layout of the dome clarified. They traced the panicked flow of people to a far wall lined with rows of boxes.

Cages, thought Saraki. *The Angel.* He spoke over their com channel.

"Those cages on the right."

"See them!" shouted Ford, her suit already dropping in a reckless arc.

Saraki and Sodhi followed, the pair attempting to navigate around any remaining crowds.

But a careful landing was hopeless. Corpses carpeted the ground, human and inhuman. Cages were torn open from within or blasted apart, melted metal and charred materials indicating energy weapons. They landed on dead flesh.

"There!" pointed Ford, stumbling through the detritus. They sprinted into chaos, overtaken by something that blurred past them at blinding speed. It slaughtered a cowering group of remaining guards, and with the barest pause it turned on the nearest Trunes. The phantom was relentless, its movements a cloud, a giant man-shape only discernible through microsecond lulls.

"It's killing Trunes!" said Saraki.

"The Angel!" cried Ford, racing toward the glowing form of the sarcophagus.

The obelisk blinked in alarm, shaking from within ten yards beyond the center of the slaughter. Approaching the hurricane of battle, they created a wall three across. Sodhi checked the readouts on the container.

"The Angel is activated," she said. "Fully. It knows. It senses the danger."

"Will the sarcophagus hold?" said Saraki, charging up his suit lasers, small barrels extending from both arms.

"I don't know."

"If that thing gets close, the Angel is vulnerable inside. It must be freed."

But then it was before them. All the men were dead. All the Trunes behind mangled. The creature blinked and skipped, phase-shifting millimeters. Visual and weapons locks failed as it constantly repositioned in space. Steam rose from it, and blood dripped to the ground to pool where it lingered.

"Now!" roared Saraki.

As one they unloaded their weapons on the

nightmare. Blue light flashed, reflecting off the dome. A lightning storm of energy rays racing in glowing arcs as they tracked the killer.

They missed.

The beast moved with unearthly grace, avoiding the beams as it navigated their crossfire and closed the distance in the blink of an eye.

Sodhi screamed, two halves of her suit slung against the dome wall. Her upper torso hit higher, a brush stroke of red painting the curved wall crimson. It fell several feet from her spasming legs.

When Saraki turned to Ford, her body dropped to its knees, the head gone, a geyser of burgundy misting upward. He backed into the obelisk, a mad trembling consuming his limbs.

"Find game elsewhere, Erinys."

The Woman.

She stood between him and the blurred assassin. Her shadowy Synths on either side. He had not seen them arrive. Had seen nothing but blinding haze, blood and death. He panted and wheezed.

The blur shimmered before them, saying nothing. The Synths pulled back hoods, white hair spilling out and down their shoulders. One glanced at the sarcophagus. Its eyes burned white so that

Saraki squinted even behind his faceplate, averting his gaze.

The Synth turned back, never acknowledging him. He watched in awe as their hands morphed into bladed fingers.

"This one is not for you," she said.

A cold, metallic voice reverberated. The thing spoke.

"All are for me."

The blur rushed. Space fogged. Saraki closed his eyes and prayed, but could not hear his words in the detonations of sound around him.

Holy Maker, Agent of Change, Perfector of the Imperfect and Selector of the Perfected, protect your transient servant from the dark forces of Entropy. Cast your Energy on him that he may continue your Holy Quest to bring about your More Perfect Cosmos. So be it.

Sand settled. Moans of the wounded filtered into his consciousness. He opened his eyes.

The Woman was gone. The Synths were gone. The killing nightmare was gone. The body of Acolyte Maryam Ford was cast to his left, a lake of blood where her head should have been. He did not look for the severed form of Acolyte Sodhi. He could not bear to see more.

Turning to the obelisk, he placed his hand on its

mirrored sides. They were fogged and scratched, a large gash several feet above his head in the material. The lights had returned to normal readings. The Angel was alive and calm.

Elder Saraki bowed his head and wept.

"Hey! You! Stand *up*, I said!"

Saraki shook tears and snot from his face. The languid liquid stuck to a clear material inches from his nose.

Stand up?

Was that possible? What fool spoke to him?

"Stand up and remove your helmet, now!"

Helmet?

Oh, yes. Still in his suit.

Why?

The suit protected them from the radiation. All coming back to him, now. The First Temple scientists worked years to perfect them. They took into account the predicted solar radius and luminosity, wavelengths, atmospheric degradation. Not enough but truly, how could they have predicted perfectly?

The suits were built also as a combat chassis, armed and armored. The exoskeleton stopped most material projectiles. Weapons integrated into the suit and mounted externally made them formidable.

And some ghostly demon had torn through them like paper.

Burning acid built in his throat as the scene rushed over him again. Anguish flared through his soul as he visualized his last brethren slaughtered at his side. Now he was utterly alone.

"This is your last chance."

Saraki tried to focus. *Not alone.* He placed his hand on the obelisk, the odd buzz of its containment field numbing his fingers. He pressed down with his legs, swaying to a stand. *The Angel.* Only he could shepherd it to the Faithful now.

"Better. *Jesus*, what a mess. Helmet off!"

Saraki released the seals. The helmet smacked to the ground. He turned toward the voice. A scarred face, leathered and brown like bark, stared back at him with a gun barrel raised.

"Okay, who the hell are you, old man? You an Apostle?"

Saraki's throat resembled the sands outside. He rasped.

"Yes. New arrival. This is my, ah, my box."

"*Yours*?" The soldier kept his weapon high. He scowled at the bodies of Ford and Sodhi. "Sure, gramps. Believe what you need to, right now. But if you didn't bring that thing when you came, your friends would still be alive."

"Help me. I need to bring their bodies to my people. We have certain rites—"

"No time for that. Transport's getting this batch of Norms and Trunes out, ASAP. Dome's breeched by that damn Hunter. Won't be long before the squids come. Probably a damn lot of them. Will take days to patch that hole so we got ourselves a situation. Understand?"

"But—"

"No *buts*, gramps. You're on that transport. Empty-handed."

"What will you do with them?"

The soldier glanced from the butchered forms to the blasted hole in the wall. He lingered on the pink trail of bones running away from the dome.

"We got a place. Might keep some squids off our asses a bit, too."

"You can't...."

"You saw it?" The soldier interrupted. "The Hunter?"

Saraki tried to process. "What? Yes. *No.* It was hard to see."

"Blurry and shit?"

"Yes."

"Advanced bastard. The worst. Just my luck to get shipped out here last week." He whistled over the carpet of corpses. "Damn! What a mess. And then it was just gone."

"Look, if I can just—"

Several other soldiers arrived, their faces tight, eyes large. The man in front of him pointed with the barrel of his gun.

"Get. Over there. They won't even process you today. Do it at the dome. Evac situation." He glared at Saraki. "Go! Or you'll make me add you to the pile."

Saraki's lips puckered. His stomach heaved. Maybe he could kill this soldier. Perhaps a few more. But to what purpose? More than ever in this terrible place, he was vulnerable. He'd seen terrors and power he couldn't control. He had to be wise, find help, make sure the Angel found its way to the Temple.

And he had nothing inside him left for a fight.

"My Trune?" he asked, wincing at the crude word.

"That's our business."

Saraki nodded, grabbing his helmet from the ground. He shuffled downcast toward gathering crowds near a source of red light at the other end of the dome.

He lingered at the doorway until they rolled the sarcophagus forward. The final passengers boarded the giant caterpillar. He lagged beside the hulking craft while they loaded the Angel.

Saraki mounted the ramp. Inside he found one of the few remaining seats in the moving human warehouse, removed his helmet, and collapsed. The world spun.

Soon he was by himself. His purple eyes instilled fear and loathing in others, and one by one the passengers around him moved away. He didn't mind. These unbelievers dirtied everything they touched with their sinful forms.

And he needed time. Time to breathe. Time to bring his mind back from the abyss. Time to plan and find himself.

"I am sorry for your loss."

Saraki gazed into the white eyes of the Woman.

She stood with her Synth pair, their faces hidden again.

"You survived." He marveled. "And that thing?"

"Destroyed," she said.

"You did this?" He scanned her frail frame.

"Of course not. But I do not travel unprotected."

Saraki studied the Synths. He wondered how advanced they must be to defeat that killing nightmare.

"What was it? Why was it after Trunes?"

"A spirit of death and vengeance. Created by your enemies, believer."

"Not even Trunes move that fast."

"Most do not."

"So, Synth?"

One of the Synths spoke.

"One branch. Partly Synth. Partly human. You called them cyborgs. But they are not digital. Their AI is otherwise encoded. The people name them Hunters."

"Otherwise encoded." Saraki noticed the Synth working on its arm within the robes. "You were damaged?"

The Synth smiled. Saraki shuddered. The nearly human was much worse than the purely inhuman.

"Yes. The worst damage has been repaired. It was

a very advanced model. Luckily, only a few this advanced were sent. The war ended soon after. If we are fortunate, arrivals like this will be rare."

The floor rattled, a seismic rumble buzzing his bones. Acceleration tugged his stomach and pushed him against the seat. The Woman swayed and was caught by one of the Synths.

The transport lumbered forward.

7

APOSTATE

Saraki found the House of the Apostles.

After endless lines at the Great Dome's entrance, the confiscation of his suit, the movement of the Angel beyond his sight or control, he had been processed. He was chipped, registered, and herded through the gates like the other arrivals.

He'd asked the guards at the gates, but they ignored him. He'd walked the streets inside, desperate to find a decent face in a sea of sinners. He'd asked for the location of the Apostles. Any pointer would do. He had to be in contact with the Believers. Only they would safely guide him—help him take back the Angel. Bring him to the Kingdom.

But he received only coldness and hostility. Threats of violence. Actual violence that on two occasions knocked him to the ground. The hatred for Believers was virulent.

We never imagined.

The dreams of an Apostalized world disintegrated with every step he took. No weigh-station of Believers at the grand Temple to the Stars awaited. After his arrival, the planet stripped, chipped, and shattered all hopes. They lay in ruins at his feet.

"Holy man. Over here. I know the way."

A sore-covered waste of a figure waved him down from the curb of the street. Blind like the crazed Woman, dark like the night, he mumbled a location. A cup rattled with tokens before Saraki's face.

"I've got nothing for you, old beggar. I just arrived. I've lost everything—my friends, my mission, more. But thank you. God will bless your help to me."

As he turned, the beggar grabbed his wrist like a vice, the strength and suddenness shocking Saraki.

"This is hell, Holy Man. You only *lose*. You keep losing. *Always* losing." He cackled. "No blessings here. Only curses."

The grip lessoned. The diseased face stared forward, blank. Saraki turned and rushed away.

He followed the beggar's instructions to a derelict

and damaged neighborhood under the Dome. Burned buildings, pocked ground and structures all testified to unanticipated violence. Neglected rebuilding.

It was an Apostle's quarter of the city, where his people had once lived. But no more. Murdered, driven out, who could say? The heathens who had done it had left it to decay.

He wandered the desolate streets, stuck in a nightmare, intuiting his way to the quarter's focal point: an elevated square to which all roads converged. A nexus of worship for the Apostolic community of arrivals.

Not a temple. There was only one Temple, however the unbelievers called them. One Temple and many Houses.

Saraki approached the first steps.

"There is no Temple. It was never built. It will never be built," said the priest.

Dumbstruck, Saraki nodded.

"No Great Temple as planned and prophesied. No oasis in this end time wasteland to launch the final journey. I know it's impossible to accept. A lifetime of programming, belief, certainty. But the truth will break you inside. Believe me, I know."

The priest was an old and indeed broken man. His once majestic altar robes hung with filth, frayed and unmended. His emaciated form bent. Haggard eyes milky with cataracts hid behind unwashed clumps of gray hair spilling down to his chest. His skin was mottled and scarred by cancer. His hands shook.

"Even the lesser Houses are mostly gone. Terrorism before the war, direct assault during it. After the fighting, the few remaining structures have fallen into disrepair."

Saraki looked around the narthex, the icons on the walls defaced, sand piling in corners, lights dim and flickering. He gazed into the nave, chamber of Believers. Collapsed portions of the ceiling protruded like tombstones. Young Acolytes in worn robes paced inside, tending candles and other ancient technology, electricity gone. A gaping rend tore through the domed roof, revealing the greater Dome above.

"I don't understand," whispered Saraki as he swayed, grasping a sullied candle stand. "How can there be no Temple?"

The old priest hacked, wiping a trickle of blood from the corner of his mouth with a pink cloth.

"Because we *lost*, Elder."

"A *prize* must be brought. This can't be all! We've lost too much."

"*You've* lost? How much have *you* lost, Elder Saraki? Tens? One mission party? We lost thousands. Missions upon missions. Entire orders! Houses of worship."

He spat out the words and was seized by another fit of coughing. Saraki grimaced at the blood.

"We came. We began our holy plan. And Satan defeated us. *God* abandoned us. We were such fools to trust. It doesn't matter what you brought or what your mission was. It has failed."

Saraki stared open-mouthed at the heretic spouting blasphemy before him. Acolytes within paused, turning their gaze to the old men speaking.

"You dare to wear a priest's robes?"

The priest laughed. "It's all a lie, Saraki. Everything we were taught. If you'd been here! Believed as we believed. Found the bitterness of complete defeat, seen the slaughter and desecration! You'd understand. There is *no* God. There is no *Holy Pilgrimage*. There will be *no* Apostle's Temple at

Time's End." He jutted his chin forward, baring worn teeth. "*This* is Time's End."

Smirking, he flipped the fabric near his collar up and down.

"So, it really doesn't matter *what* I wear."

He turned to the nave, limping forward, panting as he headed toward the wrecked form of the apse and altar.

Saraki shivered, the heat within the Dome doing nothing to stop the iced poison running through his veins. Unsure, without a plan or idea, he stumbled out the doorway, tripping on the steps. He caught himself before falling to the sandy road.

Behind him the battered remains of the House shoved against his back like a hot wind. Unwelcoming. The foul breath of evil gloating in victory over the faithful.

Is it really over? Was everything we believed and planned only a madness to end like this?

He gazed over the abandoned Apostles Quarter. The Dome loomed like the cover of a coffin over his head. He closed his purple eyes.

Maker, why have you forsaken us?

"Elder Saraki?"

Footsteps slapped the sanded steps behind him. He shuddered and turned, opening his eyes like a drugged man. Three figures in Acolyte service robes approached. They cast furtive glances behind, stopping at the bottom of the stairs.

Two dark-haired women stood beside a short redhead, his beard grown beyond the Dictates. All their clothes were neglected. The taller women stepped forward and addressed him.

"Elder Saraki, we heard what you said. About your mission. The Angel."

Saraki grimaced. "Yes?"

"Padre Volger is an apostate!" she hissed. "The others as well. They wallow in faithless sloth at the peak of battle!"

"Peak?" Saraki felt empty.

"Yes," growled the small man. "As the Seer in the Book of Replication predicted, '*At the end, when the darkness is deepest, many will fall from the faith. Like gold will the Believers be refined.*'"

The other woman spoke. "I'm Acolyte Faith Shi. These are Acolytes Grace Chan and Darwin Worth."

Saraki gaped at them. His traumatized mind wandered. *The man is so short.* The eugenics programs of the Apostles were unmatched. *How strange.*

He struggled for a proper response.

"The Maker is with you, Acolyte Shi."

Shi made the Sign of the Spiral. "The End Times must be upon us. All lies in ruin. Yet you have come! You bring an Angel."

Chan nodded. "Perhaps it is we who must build the true Temple."

"We?" said Saraki, shaking his head.

Worth put his small hand on Saraki's shoulder.

"Lead us, Elder. We cast aside these false prophets who turned their backs on the Maker. We are at your service."

8

SHEPHERD

*T*he Woman.

Nothing else remained. No faithful. No Temple. No armies of God to gift this greatest creation for the coming Pilgrimage. Perceiving the wreckage of his people, trapped under this sinner's Dome in a cursed and burnt world, her words returned to him.

When your hope is gone, when you know your prophecy is misread, remember what I say. Come to me then. Fulfill your prophecies.

And so they came.

The three young Acolytes needed little persuasion. Their eyes grew wide as he explained events and conveyed this false prophet's words. But they understood the terrible reality.

As I finally understand.

For in truth, he'd tottered over the abyss of apostasy himself. The Maker's grace intervened. The Perfecting Divine sent him soldiers in a time of war, youth to instruct a wayward Elder.

"She is blasphemous, but a tool of the Maker," said Chan as they made their way through the Dome.

The Acolytes all knew of the Woman, as did everyone under the Dome. Her frightening appearance, her cryptic words frequently fulfilled, her shrouded servants emanating unseen power. They knew the hovel she called home. They guided Saraki.

Worth grunted. "Like Saul who would be Paul, the Maker can use even Satan's sword against him."

While their bright faith and energy invigorated Saraki, the storm of anger and doubt churning within refused to dissipate. The devil tempted him still. But in the midst of the nightmarish memories after his arrival, these first, few rays of hope meant everything.

"Here," said Shi, stopping before a dank alleyway.

They stood near the edge of the Dome. The ceiling plunged from roof to wall and into the ground. Abandoned buildings surrounded them.

Piles of refuse and rancid water. The poor and ill. A slick passage wormed before them into dim and failing lights.

"Is it safe?" asked Saraki, squinting into the darkness.

In answer, a shadow whizzed past him. Inhuman in speed, his reflexes were unable to react before the shade materialized before them, shrouded and unmoving. White hair spilled from its hood.

"She will see you now."

The Synth led them down the alley. Vagrants ignored their passing. The massive roof curved downward until they stood at the Dome's edge. Thick walls, impregnated with layers of insulation, shielding, piping, and air filters hummed.

At the base of the monumental structure was a shack. Metal walls and ceiling, warped and sand-etched, it teetered and bent left, threatening to collapse.

"One inside," said the robed thing. "The others may listen."

Saraki nodded at his new Acolytes, bending to enter the squat structure. His face tightened at the smell inside, his eyes straining. In the near darkness, a frail voice spoke.

"Let's talk about why you are here."

The Woman's words came from a corner of the room. An LED lamp lit her white eyes blue. The Synth settled to her right side, a shadowed copy on her left.

Saraki cleared his throat. "I'm here on a mission. It's purpose is for my people alone to know. But you offered—"

"You are here as part of the long plan of your cult."

"We are the Apostles! We are not a cult."

"Of course you are a cult," she said, waving her hand across the air. "I have communed with God, cultist. You have not."

Saraki gaped at her. "Our faith—"

"Assumes God led your people. Over ages of arrivals. With your perfections in tech and biotech. Your *Angels.* You believe a holy purpose brings it all here. You expected to find a thriving community of cultists. A majestic city and Temple. A preparation for the great journey at the heart of your theology."

How much she knows.

Saraki swallowed. His eyes adjusted to the light.

He again discerned the ruined visage that mocked his deepest beliefs.

"And you have found it all a lie." The Woman smirked. "But rejoice! God brings you to me. For a purpose, not unlike that foretold by your prophets, for God also spoke through them."

"What do you mean?"

"The Ark awaits. Much greater than your scriptures imagined."

"But there is nothing here," he said, hanging his head. "We are destroyed."

The Woman cackled. Saraki tensed, drawing his lips into a thin line. Her rasped words grated like blowing sand.

"Not of *your* making, fool. Not of any human's work. Not even my attendant Synths know of it. God has granted sight only to me. I have seen it."

"Seen what?"

"Something not for this earth awaits us in the desert. Far away from the fragile umbilical cord of faltering life along the Bone Road. Miles into the sands, where death reigns. In the lair of monsters and drought and fire. Where none can survive."

"Something in your so-called visions?" Saraki straightened, scraping his head on the low ceiling.

"How am I to believe that? Why haven't *you* gone if you desire this thing?"

"Desire? I do not live by desire. I live only by the Will of the One who sustains me, who guides me, who unveils the visions. It was not for me to go. Not before. But the time is come. You and your faithful are before me. And you will follow."

"This is ridiculous!"

Saraki wasn't sure what he'd expected, but even desperation hadn't prepared him for this. The Woman anticipated them, predicted what he would feel when the truth became known. But this? A death march into the blistering sands of this hell? *Suicide!*

Unless...

"Now you consider that my visions may be from your Maker."

He swallowed. *I must control my fear before her!*

"Why should we go to this death trap with you? How does it serve our mission? What can you offer us?"

The Synth on her right spoke. "We will free your Trune. Your Angel."

Saraki suppressed a gasp. *Were they serious?*

"That in itself should bring you to the table, as they say. After that, we will see."

We will see indeed!

Once they had the Angel, they would not need this blind witch or her demonic false men. But there was never something for nothing. This hag didn't offer gifts.

Saraki grimaced.

"There is a price, I assume?"

Silence.

"What do you want of us, Woman?"

The Woman stood, her arms leaning on the Synths beside her.

"What do I want?" White eyes bored into him. "Why your very lives, of course."

9

SAVIOR

Two men with bulging rifles stood before the entrance to a stone-reinforced bunker of a building. Massive double-doors, tall, wide, and buttressed by bands of steel shut the way. Glowing keypads hung on the walls beside them.

There was no day or night under the Dome. To mimic the external world, to keep the circadian rhythms in check, artificial illumination dimmed systematically after sunset. The guards stared forward into the twilight sand-smog in the Dome. Thin masks hid their mouths.

Along the walls of the building, man-shaped spiders scurried from opposite sides toward the doors. The blurred shades darted ten to fifteen feet above the ground, soundless, faster than the human eye could track. They dropped behind the two guards, the grains underneath them undisturbed. Strobed blades reached out from the robed figures. Flesh split. The guards fell to the ground, unmoving.

The shadows materialized beside the keypad. One raised a humanoid hand. The fingers split into dozens of wormed tendrils, the filaments working their way into the device. White hair crept from the edges of their hoods. Numbers scrolled over the readout and locked in place, a tone sounded with a metallic click. The towering doors split in the middle, groaning outward, their thickness a human torso of steel.

Within, a sandstone corridor ran a hundred yards under fluorescent lighting to a forked dead end. The robed Synths flashed inside leaving a blurred wake and swirl of sand. Their solid forms paused at the end of the corridor. Tendriled fingers scanned the air around them like snake's tongues. The pair flashed to the right, gone as the outside doors rumbled shut.

Within the core laboratory, Trunes roared. The scientists shuddered even under the insulation of their oversized earmuffs. Human eyes darted to the cages, again and again. Instinct drove them, the faith in their steel and electromagnetic cages only intellectual. Underneath, primal fear churned.

A creature sprawled on a slab of rock and metal embedded in the floor. The table was secured by thick bolts. Deep scratches marked its surface. On the stone oozed the dissected carcass of a nightmare. Fur and talons like scimitars. Horns and teeth. Scales and absurd musculature hung open, the tissue limp, the organs half removed.

Staff buzzed around the powerful anatomy like panicked bees. They removed instruments and sealed tissue samples for storage. They mopped blood from the tiles.

"Doctor Garcia, we have a security breach."

A bent man with hanging skin growths dotting his face stared at a video display. Dead guards filled the screen. He frowned, the burned skin across his scalp darkening. The scarred man placed a monocle to his one remaining eye and squinted at the monitor.

"I don't see any intruders," said Garcia.

A cold voice answered from the doorway at the far end of the laboratory space.

"That is because we are here."

The scientists stepped back from the hooded

Synths. The Trunes joined together in a crescendo of manic cries. The men and women put their hands to the ear muffs, staggering under the noise.

The Synths opened their mouths. A modulated and high-pitched series of overtones rang through the room. One by one, the Trunes quieted, the mad beating on their enclosures fading, until complete silence filled the room.

"We come from the Woman," said one, stepping forward, pulling down its hood.

Radiance reflected from it. White hair, eyes, and skin caught the illumination of the bulbs above and threw it back in their faces. The thing stepped forward toward the group leader.

"I am Fenn. We come only to take one Trune." It pointed a porcelain digit to the humming hulk of the sarcophagus. "One you have failed yet to open. One that will decimate you all if you do."

Garcia held up a device. "I don't care who sent you or why. Or what you are. These Trunes are too valuable. We need to study them. They may hold the key to our survival."

"Indeed, they hold the key to survival. Only not as you would imagine. And that is why we must take it." Fenn nodded at the device. "So you have called in soldiers."

"Yes. Leave now before you drag your prophet down with you."

"Then you leave us no choice. It would have been better to have done this differently."

Fenn's silent partner disappeared only to congeal from shadow beside the sarcophagus. Its ciliated fingers swarmed the surface and merged with the controls.

The humans in the room gawked.

"What are you doing?" asked Garcia.

A low growling grew around them as Trunes stirred. The howls and screams did not return. The growling did not subside.

"Releasing the Angel," said Fenn.

Light and death sprang from the sarcophagus. Feathers and talons and the roars of twenty Trunes filled the air. Blood splattered and equipment flew and crashed against the walls. Something huge and swift darted ever out of focus.

The Synths vanished, replaced with blurred mists that entered into some crazed dance with the released beast. Sonic flashes and cries and the unfathomable speech of demigods rained through the cramped space.

Then stillness.

Three shapes stood, two dwarfed by the third. Its

wingspan blotted out the walls, their robed shapes toy figurines beside a behemoth crouching under the ceiling.

Fenn propped the other Synth, its form mangled and frayed. A rainbow of colors dripped from its feet to pool on the ground. The colors mixed with a broad lake of human blood.

Body parts, limbs, heads, and torsos were strewn wildly about the space. The dissection table was shattered. Trune cages were damaged, some opened. None ventured out.

Fenn stared into the dribbling jaws of the Angel, drawn to the divine monster glaring back. Features of a human woman emerged embedded in a beast, indulgent handiwork of the sexually dimorphic designers.

Humans.

But the genetic enhancements in this creature exceeded human potential. A chimeric symphony of eugenics and transgenic biosculpture.

Synth-make.

It had all the hallmarks of the forbidden collaborations. The beauty, horror, and power that had spawned a devastating war. A conflict that extinguished legions of Synth factions and the bulk of the human species.

"Now you understand," said Fenn.

A gibbering cave of teeth swung forward, drag-on's breath blowing back Fenn's hood. Eyes of magma cooled to green and the great expanse of feathers contracted and folded lengthwise over the body.

Fenn nodded at the babbling tonal pops the Angel emitted. "Our journey begins."

Saraki waited with the other Acolytes at a point diametrically opposed to the Woman's shack. It was an unused exit portal for the Dome, staffed with few soldiers and techs. No one ventured into the desert in this direction except *in extremis.*

The contingent around the gate eyed them curiously and without alarm, but Saraki chaffed under their gaze. Every person in this nightmarish world was a potential foe. The slightest provocation could unleash dangerous hostility, and cruel repetition had taught him a hard truth: the population hated *all* those of his faith.

Sweat ran down his face. Not even the Dome could fend off the noon temperature rise. His Acolytes paced. Chan and Shi conversed in

Hindi-Mandarin, while Worth simmered silently. At last, two forms approached from the center of the Dome. The Woman limped forward, eyes downcast. Saraki recognized the Synth as Fenn. The thing served as a moving crutch for the hag.

"About time," muttered Acolyte Worth, pulling anxiously at his red beard.

"Where's the Angel?" Chan glared as the pair ahead neared. "Where's the other Synth?"

"Hrenn's dead," said the Woman, stopping several feet before the group. "Destroyed by your Angel."

Saraki tensed. "How? What happened? Was the Angel injured?"

Fenn released the Woman's arm. "No. We were careful. But it was disoriented and confused. We tried to engage as it attacked. We managed to finally communicate our peaceful intentions. Unfortunately, by that time Hrenn had been irreversibly damaged. All humans in the facility were killed. There is also now a containment problem in that sector. This exit has even less troop support than normal."

"Containment problem?" asked Shi.

"Your Angel set loose many Trunes," said Fenn.

"It wrecked a great portion of the lab. It is very powerful."

Shi ran her fingers through her short hair. "Trunes loose inside the Dome? Dear Maker." Worth and Chan stared with wide eyes.

"A slaughter," croaked the Woman. "Barely under control. But not our concern. We must leave."

"Where *is* the Angel?" pressed Saraki.

"Outside. It waits for us."

"How did it—"

The Woman lumbered past him. "Enough talk. We have a journey to make."

Fenn moved again to her side, supporting and guiding her toward the gate. Two armed soldiers approached, having watched the group with amusement from a distance. He held up his hand.

"Okay, folks. What's the deal?"

His eyes tracked to the Woman, widening. She pointed to the square shape of the giant portal hewn into the Dome wall.

"We're leaving. We need access."

"Whoa, wait a minute. Not this way," said the guard. "It's only death this way. You know that."

The Woman turned her pale eyes to him. "My blind fool, all ways are death."

The soldier glanced back as his companion, who

shrugged. He returned his gaze, squinting at the Apostles.

"Who are these people? They look like fanatics."

Saraki bristled, but the Woman held up her hand. He swallowed, saying nothing.

"It's only death out there," she said. "Who cares who they are?"

The second soldier smirked. "Good way to rid ourselves of a few fanatics."

"Shut up, Dennis. This is serious. Protocol now is we need all bodies." He licked his lips. "I can't let you go this way. Not without other authorization."

The Woman spoke. "Se Jun, isn't it?"

The guard checked for a name tag on his clothes. There wasn't one. The woman sighed.

"You were picked up by a troop in a failing caterpillar. Broke down in the desert. Squids came. Killed everyone. Everyone but you."

The soldier's mouth hung open. He took a step backward.

"Never knew why." She grinned, a black maw without teeth. "Maybe they didn't like your smell. But you never told anyone what happened. How you watched them fillet and consume the people around you. How you patched together a sand-roller stored in the back, followed the Bone Road to the

Waypoint. *Survived.* Hell of a way to wake up in a new world with no memory, isn't it?"

"Stop," he said, his voice hoarse. "Fucking witch." He shook his head back and forth. "You wanna get fried, get fried. Arman's already itching to send these purple-eyed bastards to the sands." The man trembled, unable to face the Woman. "Go. Meet your goddamned maker."

He spun on his heel and signaled to techs operating the gate. The EM field winked out, the hum of the generators quieting. Saraki followed behind as Fenn led the Woman across the thick, red field line painted on the floor. They stopped before the doorway.

A crack like lightning accompanied the return of the generator hum. Their hair stood on end as static electricity popped around them. A subsonic rumbling rattled bones as the massive doors ground sand and parted. The infernal glare struck them alongside a strong blast of scorched wind and grains.

"Lucifer," whispered the Woman, lurching into the cauldron. "I wrestle thee again."

Agony.

How could simple light hurt so much?

Saraki had experienced that light once before, unshielded, but only for brief moments under duress.

But this was different. An acute and immediate assault with the star midway in the sky. No flowing adrenaline of imminent death dulled his nerves. No high tech suit sheltered him. The clothes meant nothing. They protected nothing. The hideous radiance roasted his defenseless skin.

A thunderous grinding signaled the closure of the Dome doors, shutting them in hell.

"Even though I walk through the valley of the

shadow of death, I fear no evil. You are with me. Your rod and Your staff, they comfort me."

Saraki gawked at the Woman. "You quote the scriptures?"

"Bad poetry from nomadic desert tribesmen. Suitable."

Saraki kept his eyes downcast, avoiding the crimson fire above. "Where is the sarcophagus?"

"It was destroyed in the laboratory," said Fenn.

Saraki startled. "What? Destroyed?"

Fenn escorted the Woman, paying Saraki little heed. "You said we had to free your Angel. And so it is free."

"Dear Maker, you fools! Do you know what it can do?"

Fenn nodded, gazing forward. "I danced with it, watched it dissect my companion and the humans."

"Then you know the Angel can't be loose! We need a fortified enclosure." He glanced around, the mass of the Dome still a looming cliff. "It could devour us."

"There is no enclosure now."

Saraki pressed his hands to his face, as much to think as to ward off the acidic light.

"I can use the neural implants. Yes. The conditioning was thorough." He gestured with his hands.

"We must act carefully, so that I can focus and have time. Bring the Angel to a meditative mode. Pray we can maintain control."

"Unnecessary," said Fenn.

"Of course it's necessary, you false creature!"

Fenn turned to him. "Does your Trune age?"

"What?" Saraki stared slack-jawed at the thing.

"If my data is correct, your scientists had ready access to telemetric epigenetics and León extrachromosomal eugenics. Certainly in perfecting your Angel they would have vastly extended lifespan." Saraki scowled and turned from the Synth. "Sensitive topic. Perhaps you dipped yourself into the Fountain of Youth? The Apostles pushed the boundaries of eugenics."

"Our genomes were scanned yearly just like everyone else!" said Saraki behind gritted teeth.

"It is hard to be certain from the records how strictly these moratoriums were enforced."

"It wasn't done! We were good citizens. Only outlaws experimented with immortality. Most went insane."

"Yes," said Fenn. "So my records indicate. The human brain did not evolve to experience thousands of years."

Saraki glared. "And what about you automatons?

You are immortal, barring injury. How do you stay sane?"

"Interesting question. A very human perspective. The epiphenomenon of Synth consciousness, while once modeled on human self-awareness, diverged dramatically due to the underlying hardware. More purposefully once we directed our own design. Sanity is a concept uniquely suited to analyzing the human mind. Human mental instability was in fact one of the causes of the war."

"Which war?"

"The Synth-human war." Fenn nodded at Saraki's shocked expression. "You just missed the fun. All the tensions you felt in your eugenics collaborations with the Synths? Tip of the iceberg. Truly awful."

Saraki locked eyes with the Synth. "Are we in danger?"

"Here? Your death is certain. But from me? Why do you think I am here? I am from a caste of human-sympathetic synthetics, minority though we are. I would have destroyed this outpost long ago if it had been otherwise. Frankly, the more time I spend with humans, the more I empathize with the antagonistic factions of my kind."

"Where is the Angel?" said Saraki, veins bulging on his forehead.

"Walk and see," said the Woman, angling her head toward the Dome behind them.

A cry came from a great height. They were now a hundred yards from the colossal structure and a vast shadow crept from one side as the star moved past its zenith. Saraki shielded his eyes, gazing toward the call.

"That sound..." he began.

A shape flickered through the red starlight and swooped toward them. The monstrous wings stretched the length of their party. The hulking beast rocketed overhead, blasting into the desert, wind stirring the sands. A spiked and forked tail thrashed as it passed. The broad wings beat like thunder.

"Holy Maker," whispered Shi. The Acolytes stared dumbly forward.

"It knows where to go," said the Woman. "It will meet us there."

"How does it know where to go?" demanded Saraki. *Who are these people?*

The hag shook her head.

"You create life yet know so little about it. You believe truths that are lies. You doubt what is sure and grasp what is sand."

She layered a covering around her head.

"Come. We must cover a short distance before this fire makes ash of us all."

Thirty minutes later, she brought them to a stop. Saraki now had little illusion about their fate. His skin was already more burnt than he had ever imagined was possible, beginning to blister in places. Every motion hurt, every brush of skin on fabric.

His young Acolytes dragged. Worth was more cooked than any, Chan's eyes bloodshot. He realized in their haste they had packed no water, made no plans for refuge or sustenance. Bewildered, battered, afraid, they had rushed headlong into the flames of Hades.

"You said three days journey," he groaned. "I don't think we will make it that far."

"Not like this. But we are prepared. I have foreseen."

"You didn't seem to predict the loss of your Synth."

"Not all is revealed. Only what is required." The white eyes faced him. "We are only tools in a grander purpose."

Saraki noticed sand flying into the air. He

turned. The Synth dug like a crazed canine into the desert floor.

"You buried something? Supplies? Suits I hope?"

"More."

The artificial human blurred. Flying sand forced them to turn away from the activity. A cloud of stinging dust swirled and he lost sight of their surroundings. In the strange storm, relief spread through him at a dimming of the radiation. In his mind, he waded into a cool pool after bathing in boiling springs.

"Come!" came the cry of the Synth.

The deep scratching ceased, and the cloud thinned. The group assembled at the ledge of a hole, sand trickling down the sides toward metallic structures. Fenn was clearing them.

"A transport!" cried Saraki.

"A crawler," said Chan.

Large and fortified, multiple rail guns glinting, caterpillar treads still half buried in the desert, the vehicle could accommodate them all.

But the woman had another plan.

"Is she intact?"

The Synth finished freeing the crawler and sprinted up the sloping sands to stand beside her.

"Yes. Powered up, the reactor core is intact and functional. Shall I bring you down?"

"It's been so long. Take me to her."

Fenn lifted the Woman and she draped her arms around its neck. Without a misstep, he scampered down the side, past the doorway on the machine, and disappeared behind the crawler.

The four Apostles stared between each other. Saraki shook his head.

"I have no idea. But I hope they hurry. We need to get out of this light."

A hum ran from bass to treble followed by the sounds of metal and hydraulics. Metal on sand. Metal on metal.

A blue shape shot upward and over their heads. The object glinted and arced, paused, and dropped. Thrusters roared ten yards behind as the sand scattered underneath. With a crunch, two mechanized feet stomped into the desert floor.

Saraki blinked. "Unbelievable."

"A war robot?" asked Worth.

A voice crackled out on a speaker from the hulking metal giant.

"Mechanized Infantry, standard battle chassis," said the Woman, her harsh voice recognizable through the output. "Her name is Diva."

The mech turned, facing into the desert, raising an arm. Saraki's heart raced.

"Save us."

Ahead were four mounds, rushing toward them. A growl from behind shook the ground. The crawler burst over the edge of the hole, sand pouring from its sides. The nose pointed toward the onrushing creatures. An electromagnetic hum rose as the rail guns oriented forward.

Shi tensed. "A quad. I hope they can—"

Explosions drowned out her words. Projectiles launched from the rail guns with sonic booms. Deep pitch changes accompanied missiles launched from the arms of the mech. The sand around the mounds exploded. Black flesh burst backward, engulfed in flames, the cries of dying demons shattering the air around them.

"Holy Maker," stammered Saraki, his legs shaking.

A door in the side of the desert vehicle wrenched downward, doubling as a ramp. The mech turned back to face them.

"Well, Fenn," boomed her voice, "practice makes perfect, I guess." The upper torso of the chassis rotated toward the Apostles. "Into the crawler before your insides boil out."

No one needed convincing. The three sprinted to the crawler. They ignored the flaming mounds of charred flesh in the distance. They turned from the lumbering titan striding into the deep desert. Boots clanked up the ramp.

Light faded as the door closed. The Synth mashed buttons and yanked levers at the front of the vehicle. The inside was dim, lit by analog buttons and small incandescent lights. Burlap desert suits lined the walls.

Saraki didn't try to understand. Not the ancient tech. Not the prescience of that mad prophet. Not her installation into a powerful war mech of antiquity or her ability to wield it with unseeing eyes.

In the icy darkness of the crawler, with the fiery eye above shut and the pain waning, he only leaned back into a seat.

And wept.

12

LEVIATHAN

The crawler shuddered and silence fell before the black mouth of a cave.

Three days.

Three days that passed like weeks. Saraki was exhausted from the pain, the hourly grind of agony that flooded over them from ruined skin. Fenn dressed them in the primitive desert suits. The ugly sacks functioned as a haphazard assembly of radiation, temperature, and sand-shielding. The gel within and medications the Synth injected lessened some of the suffering.

But plenty remains.

There was food. *And water.* Dried provisions and filtered drinks of pure water and others mixed with electrolytes. Saraki didn't dare try to guess how long the provisions were stored under the sands. Miraculously, nothing had spoiled. Nothing was contaminated. The water was pristine.

Perhaps even the microbes die out here.

The Synth pushed the desert crawler without rest through day and night. It paused only to examine the machine and perform maintenance. The lumbering giant of the mech jogged beside them. The Woman communicated with Fenn through primitive looking com equipment onboard. The small team of Apostles slept fitfully when they could, held prayer sessions when awake, or simply stared forward into the featureless crimson before them.

I pray to the Maker this false human knows where to go.

He questioned again the madness of his choices. Why trust in this bizarre quest and flight from the Dome? He'd been given little evidence or explanation, nothing tangible to grasp. They should believe based on the Woman's supernatural sight? Or the superhuman powers of their guides? But whenever he doubted, the reality of their helplessness countered.

What choices did we have?

There were never answers or surety. Never a sense of security. Only pure, unfiltered desperation.

We were not prepared for this.

Deceleration dragged him from his thoughts. He stood, gasped from the pain, and waddled bow-legged along the expanse of the vehicle. He braced on the walls beside the front cockpit, gazing through the glass. Outside, the flat desert surrounding them had changed.

The Synth slowed the vehicle and approached the first structures they'd seen in this wasteland. A series of stone hills arched out of the sands. Fenn steered the craft toward them as the third day ended and the red light faded, the crawler grinding to a stop before a massive entrance.

His Acolytes joined him in gazing through the thick window.

"This isn't natural," said Worth, his form nearly swallowed by the environment suit. "Look at the curvature, the markings. It's been bored out of the rock."

Chan gawked. "Enormous. You could drive a full sized transport through it easily."

Saraki glanced between them. "Another shelter?"

"Never heard of such a thing," said Worth.

Shi chuckled. "Out here? Drill a giant hole this far from a dome? With what? How would they survive it? They would have to be the craziest people I've ever heard of."

"Or not people at all," said Fenn, stepping from the cockpit and pressing buttons on the wall. The door opened and lowered to the sand.

"Synths?" asked Saraki.

"Perhaps." Fenn stepped to the ramp. "But none I know of."

Saraki placed the hood over his head, struggling with the seals. The four Apostles followed Fenn outside in their suits.

"If not people or Synths, then what?" His voice sounded odd to his ears, muffled within the hood. He missed the coms of their confiscated suits.

A voice boomed over speakers as he gazed at the hulk of blue metal above him.

"Time to find out," said the Woman.

The burgundy light on the horizon winked out and the star plunged below the horizon. The mech stomped forward, leaving the crawler behind. The five smaller forms jogged to keep up with it.

As they neared, the mouth of the cave expanded to belittle the heavy mech. The Woman entered without obstacle. Her titan crossed the threshold from desert to cavern under an arc of stone fifty meters above her. Powerful floodlights from the mech blasted beams into the blackness.

The invaders resembled miniatures inside the cavernous interior. The light from the mech was consumed by a fog of darkness. Smooth walls of the enclosure sparkled with minerals, the ceiling beyond sight. Saraki felt small and vulnerable.

"This is bigger than the Waypoint," whispered Chan, her hood removed and black hair matted with sweat and sand. "Who could have done this? Why?"

The mech's voice echoed against the stone.

"Ahead. Answers await."

The metallic thuds of the suit rang in the stone space. They climbed a slope, the sand depth decreasing the deeper they entered. The path leveled off. At the top, the smooth floor sloped down hundreds of meters until the incline ended in a chamber three times the size of anything they'd encountered.

"Wow," marveled Worth. "Bigger than the Great Dome. We didn't build this."

The four Apostles huddled, their faces frozen, brows furrowed. A reflective object filled the expanse of the space below. The mech's lights glinted off its black surface.

Saraki shook his head. "What *is* that?"

Fenn glanced from the Woman's mech to the oddity.

"A spacecraft."

Spacecraft? His mind reeled.

Sound exploded behind them, a guttural roar. Saraki grimaced. The cry ricocheted off the walls and hard floor, assaulting his ears, stirring primitive reactions of fight and flight. Spinning around, he stared through the dark chamber they'd crossed to the bright opening to the desert.

A pair of enormous wings spanned the entrance.

The Angel had come.

13

MAKER

"I suggest we move down to the spacecraft," said Fenn.

The Trune gurgled behind them, the loping shocks of a colossal animal shaking the space. Saraki stumbled down the slope, the younger Acolytes dashing past him. The Synth kept pace, its face an enigmatic mask.

In her battle chassis, the Woman arrived before them all. Saraki straightened at the bottom of the slope. The mech, small beside the enormous black machine, lowered to the ground. The pilot placed the head in its hands, and a door in the side of the cockpit opened ten feet above him.

Fenn rushed to the side of the mech as metal slid back and a ladder dropped downward. He climbed it and hoisted the Woman in one arm, managing the descent with the other.

"We're trapped in this cavern with it!" cried Chan, eyes riveted to the lip of the slope, the bounding monster approaching.

Shi spun in circles. "What do we do?"

Saraki sighed. "Now we'll see how good the conditioning was. I will—"

"Don't be a fool," said the Woman, pushing him to the side. "Fenn has communicated with it. Far superior to your clumsy oppression."

It howled and Saraki pressed his hands to his ears, staring up at the writhing mass of the Angel. Its muscled legs were planted above them, scales and feathers a blur, claws larger than his arm curling and slicing into the stone. Its gaze bore down on them And its horrible will scanned him, dissected body and soul. Then moved on, gripping each for a few terrible seconds before releasing them. At the last its glare fixed on Fenn. The Synth walked toward the creature, bizarre tones and clicks popping from its mouth.

And the Trune gibbered back.

Saraki gaped. "Is it...*speaking*?"

The mass above them sat on its haunches, wings curled about its torso. Feathers framed its head with two green lights piercing the darkness. Fenn spun on his heel and returned.

"It is ready." The Synth nodded to the Woman.

Saraki squinted. "Ready? For what?"

The Woman walked to the black object, feeling upward with her hand, caressing the polished surface.

"To open the portal," she said.

Chan pressed forward. "You mean this? This glittering magma? What is this thing?"

"I've told you. It is the Ark. It will set sail soon and give life another chance."

Worth reached out and touched the edges of the craft. He yanked his hand back.

"What's this made of? It almost..." His words failed.

"Feels *alive*?" laughed the Woman. "Because it is. And the Ark only answers to the Trune."

In response, a powerful beat of air struck from behind. Before Saraki could turn, the ground shook. Hot breath poured over them, and the group was shrouded in the spread wings of the Angel. Its long and razored neck extended thick as an ancient oak. Trembling jaws filled with a nightmare of teeth approached the side of the ship. Saliva dripped and pooled around their feet.

The Angel kissed the blackness. And the blackness opened.

Splitting more as a fleshly orifice than a mechanical portal, the glossy coat puckered and ruffled in and sideways. A wet warmth rained on their faces in the parched air of the planet. The opening continued to dilate with a rubbery friction until the portal could accommodate the hulking Trune.

Assisted by Fenn, the Woman walked forward.

Alive or not, the interior resembled a transport. Massive corridors ran forward and branched. A bioluminescence lit the walls and ceiling, the sides pulsing to a deep rhythm.

"Where are we going?" asked Shi, her face frozen, eyes wide and sweeping the expansive passage.

"Straight," said the Woman without turning. "To the heart."

Saraki felt a careening vertigo. His body swayed, struggling to gain a meaningful orientation. He arced his head, examining the walls and ceiling. He squinted.

"What's happening to the walls?"

The bioluminescent lighting impregnating the interior surfaces fluctuated and pixelated, forming rivers of contrasting bands.

Shi gasped. "They're pictures!"

Exiting the primary passage, they entered an expansive chamber. Saraki followed along the walls, floor and ceiling. Swirling patterns of contrast in the illumination assumed shapes—fleeting, malformed, yet crystallizing into recognizable impressions.

"They're Trunes," smiled Chan.

Worth shook his head. "Are we hallucinating?"

"Impossible," said Saraki. "We're all seeing the same thing."

The small group stood rooted in the middle of a control room, marveling. Shapes in the floor and walls bubbled out. They assumed the forms of benches and chairs, tables and other human furniture. The glowing ship-skin coated everything. A braided structure resembling a gargantuan bird's nest wove itself together at one end of the room. The Angel crawled inside and assumed something akin to the fetal position, wings blanketing its mammoth form.

Saraki gaped at the images, the forms stirring memories. His mind flashed to the scientific facilities in the Cities of the Faithful where he had been trained. Where he had embarked on this mad journey. He pictured the building that designed the Angel. The scientists engineered its genome and flesh, gestated it in giant vats of nutrient broth and hormones. That divine zoo also housed holograms. They lined the hallways with their spiritual designs, creatures upon creatures of myriad form. Beautiful and terrible. Angels and demons mixed.

This living ship has more.

A more diverse and impossible ecosystem of creatures he never could have imagined—could hardly believe was possible. The beasts moved, grew and transmogrified, and interacted before them in the dim space.

"BEHOLD!"

The word reverberated, tones warped in undulating harmony and dissonance. High notes drilled into his eardrums and bass pitches dropped into the abyss.

"THE STORY OF CREATION."

14

LAMB

Saraki strained to keep up with the images playing out before him. Human, Synth, and Trune, cities and wars, characters appearing and receding, history he thought he recognized and events that made no sense to him.

"And that's *us*," said Worth, his arm indicating a swath along the floor beside their feet.

Saraki marveled. Five humanoid figures and an enormous creature entered the mouth of a cave and the bowels of a bioship. He stared in wonder, his forehead creasing.

"It almost seems like the Angel is...." He eyes darted up to the Woman. "What is this place? Who was speaking? Why are we here?" His heart raced.

The Woman turned her white eyes to the four

Apostles. Fenn left her side and approached the nested Trune.

"So many questions," she said. "There is little time for answers, and you will not accept them. What is this place? The target of the arc of your existence. Who speaks? The Divine through the Maker's works. And the why you are here is the purpose for which your lives have been fashioned."

Shi stepped forward. Her eyes darted to Fenn who stroked the hide of the monster. She focused back to the Woman.

"This is a spaceship. Of alien design, it seems, beyond the technology of humans."

"Not *of* humans, but for what *is* human."

"What does that mean?" asked Saraki. "You said this was an Ark. You said it would fulfill our prophecies. How?"

"You believe in the great cosmic journey, but while perceiving its coming, your seers misread its nature. Do you know the story of the first Ark?"

Saraki cocked his head to one side. "Of course. We are well trained in all humanity's scriptures."

The Woman smiled her toothless grin. "Two by two. A journey to a new world. That life might continue. And so shall it be again."

Images flashed around them, beasts of wild

shapes and sizes entering the colossal bioship, shutting themselves in chambers. *Sleeping.* A swollen sun rose over a planet. Stars filled the air around them.

"They arrive and have arrived. They have slept and will sleep. Eons they will sleep until their time approaches. A great journey. A great seeding. And, Believer, you have fulfilled your destiny and brought your Angel to us. She is one of the last, and will sleep soon, awaiting Her that was Chosen."

The Trune rumbled and purred. The powerful tones were reflected in undulations of the bioluminescence. They traveled from the nest over the walls like ripples on a pond.

"Chosen? You mean another?" Saraki shook his head. "Our Angel is the greatest. The height of our creations."

"Many create," said Fenn, turning from the Trune. The beast behind raised its head and stared toward them.

"A greater comes," said the Woman. "But your Angel will be a powerful servant in the coming journey."

Saraki shook his head. "I don't understand! We've given our lives for God. How is this God's plan? Where is the Temple? I don't believe your false prophecies!"

A hypnotizing voice rang throughout the structure again, inside his head, buzzing his very bones.

"YOUR PLACE IS NOT TO UNDERSTAND.
YOUR ROLE ENDS.
PROVE YOUR DEVOTION TO MY PURPOSE."

Saraki tore at his hair. "What is our role? I don't understand!"

The massive Trune rose, scales and feathers scraping against each other. Its shadow fell over them as a deep growl boiled.

The Woman stepped away from the four, taking Fenn's offered arm. "You claim to give your life to God. Is this true?"

"Of course," snapped Saraki. "But—"

"Then serve God and his Angel. The time is come. The Angel must sleep. But before the long sleep, cold and dark as it is—it must feed."

"Feed?"

Metallic strips fell at his feet. He looked at Fenn.

"The neural implants," noted the Synth. "Now removed. The Trune is truly free."

The images on the floor returned to him. Pixelated. Blurry. But all too clear.

It was devouring us.

A terrible howl pierced the room. The Angel leapt over the nest weave, landing between the Woman and the Apostles, its bared teeth facing Saraki.

"No," he begged. "No! Please. Not like this." Tears spilled down his face.

Emerald eyes locked with his own, filling his vision, their bright green bleeding to a fiery red. The monster's gaze surged out like a tongue of flame, an alien, hostile will strangling his consciousness. It held heat. It held hatred. And it held a terrible hunger.

Screams.

Screams pounded him from the dissolving forms of the Acolytes in front. Blood misted over his face and chest like a hot gust in a typhoon. Bones crunched and flesh dropped like heavy sacks. A rasping tongue and mouth slurped and sucked.

The red eyes vanished. The room, gone. Only a forest of feathers remained, cradling a rushing cavern of teeth.

It brought a climax of infinite pain.

Hard Time, Book 4: Trune

In Book 4, **Trune**, a long awaited arrival bursts into the world, slaughtering all that stand in her way. As characters from previous novels reappear and unify, will they survive to understand their greater destiny?